T5-CVG-970

AMICUS ILLUSTRATED • AMICUS INK

# DO YOU REALLY WANT TO MEET
# A LION?

WRITTEN BY CARI MEISTER    ILLUSTRATED BY DANIELE FABBRI

Amicus Illustrated and Amicus Ink
are imprints of Amicus
P.O. Box 1329
Mankato, MN 56002
www.amicuspublishing.us

Copyright © 2016 Amicus. International copyright reserved in all countries. No part of this book may be reproduced in any form without written permission from the publisher.

Library of Congress Cataloging-in-Publication Data
Meister, Cari, author.
 Do you really want to meet a lion? / by Cari Meister ; illustrated by Daniele Fabbri.
     pages cm. — (Do you really want to meet...?)
 Summary: "A child goes on a safari in Africa and observes lions hunting and lions' behavior in their pride"— Provided by publisher.
 Audience: K to grade 3.
 ISBN 978-1-60753-735-9 (library binding)
 ISBN 978-1-60753-839-4 (ebook)
 ISBN 978-1-68152-009-4 (paperback)
 1. Lion—Juvenile literature. 2. Tanzania–Juvenile literature. I. Fabbri, Daniele, 1978– illustrator. II. Title.
 QL737.C23M454 2016
 599.757—dc23                          2014036642

Editor          Rebecca Glaser
Designer        Kathleen Petelinsek

Printed in the United States of America at Corporate Graphics in North Mankato, Minnesota.

HC  10 9 8 7 6 5 4 3 2 1
PB  10 9 8 7 6 5 4 3 2 1

## ABOUT THE AUTHOR

Cari Meister is the author of more than 120 books for children, including the *Tiny* (Penguin Books for Young Readers) series and *Snow White and the Seven Dogs* (Scholastic, 2014). She lives in Evergreen, Colorado, with her husband John, four sons, one horse, and one dog. You can visit Cari online at *www.carimeister.com*.

## ABOUT THE ILLUSTRATOR

Daniele Fabbri was born in Ravenna, Italy, in 1978. He graduated from Istituto Europeo di Design in Milan, Italy, and started his career as a cartoon animator, storyboarder, and background designer for animated series. He has worked as a freelance illustrator since 2003, collaborating with international publishers and advertising agencies.

So you say you want to meet a lion.
Not in the zoo, but in real life?

Did you know that lions are ferocious
hunters? They have sharp teeth and powerful
jaws that rip their prey into bite-size chunks.

Lions are also clever. They work in groups to
surround and attack animals much larger than
themselves. Do you *really* want to meet a lion?

Okay, then. Pack your bags—and a book. It will
take a whole day to get to Serengeti National Park
in Tanzania, Africa. It will be worth it, though.

The park is home to elephants, rhinos, leopards,
crocodiles, Cape buffalo, impalas, giraffes, hyenas,
and, of course, the king of beasts—the lion!

Ah, here is your safari guide. He knows
his way around and can keep you safe.
Yikes! Was that a lion?

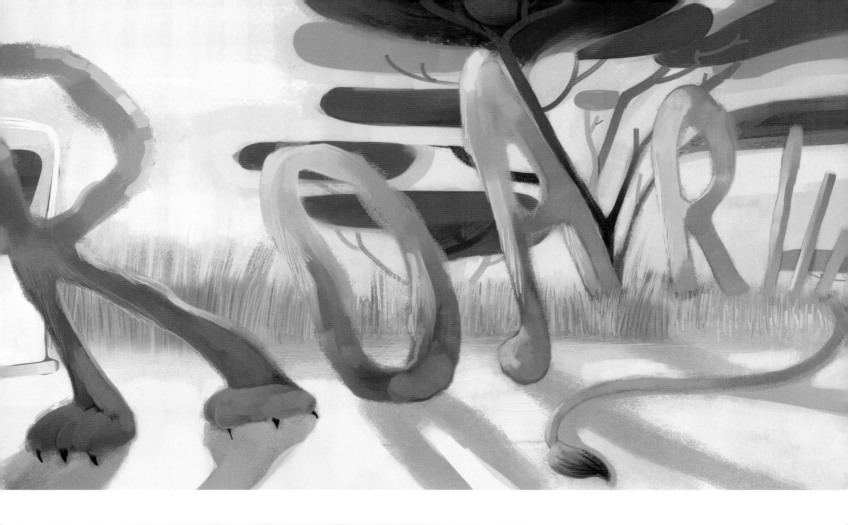

A lion's roar can be heard from over 5 miles (8 km) away. Lions roar to call to other lions in their group, or pride. Sometimes a roar warns intruders—like other male lions—to stay away.

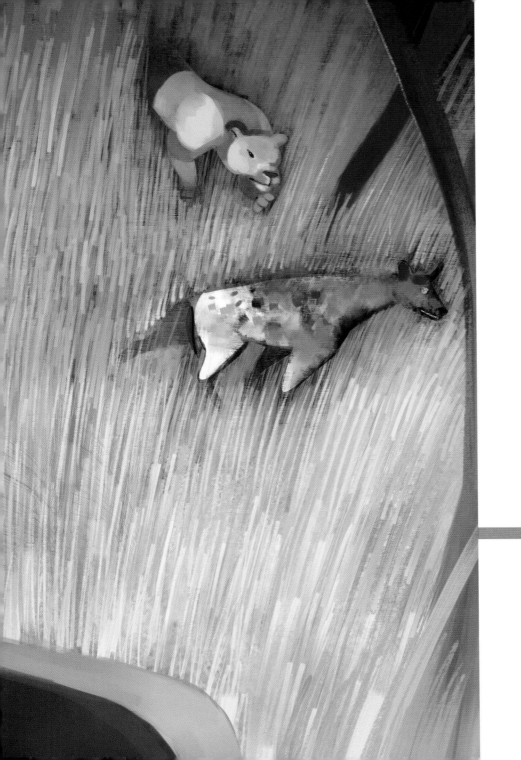

Night is the perfect time to watch lions hunt. Put on your special night vision goggles. Look! Over there! The lionesses are stalking a hyena. They pounce . . .

. . . but the hyena gets away. Lionesses do most of the hunting, but they are not always successful. They miss more than half of the things they try to catch. That's why they hunt in groups.

These lions have been following a buffalo herd for hours.
Cape buffalo are big and can kill a lion with their horns.
But the lionesses have a strategy.

They separate a weak buffalo from the rest of the herd.

They have chosen their victim—an old female with a limp.

The herd abandons the buffalo and the lions swarm in.

The lionesses roar to their pride. All the lions come to feast. But look at that! The lionesses caught the water buffalo, but the male lion gets to eat first! He gorges himself. When he's done, the lionesses eat next. The cubs get the leftovers.

Did you see enough for tonight?
It's getting late.

We'll go on safari again
tomorrow. Sweet dreams.

Wake up! There's another pride down by the river. There they are! Just "lion" around. Lions nap about 20 hours every day. Want to curl up with the cuddly wild cats?

No, I didn't think so.

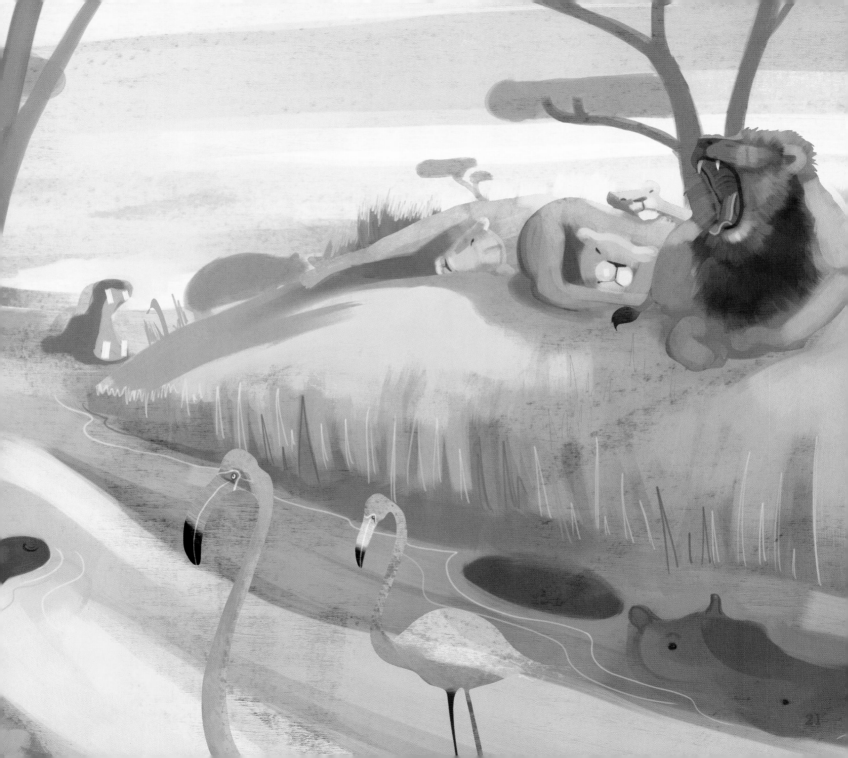

# WHERE DO LIONS LIVE?

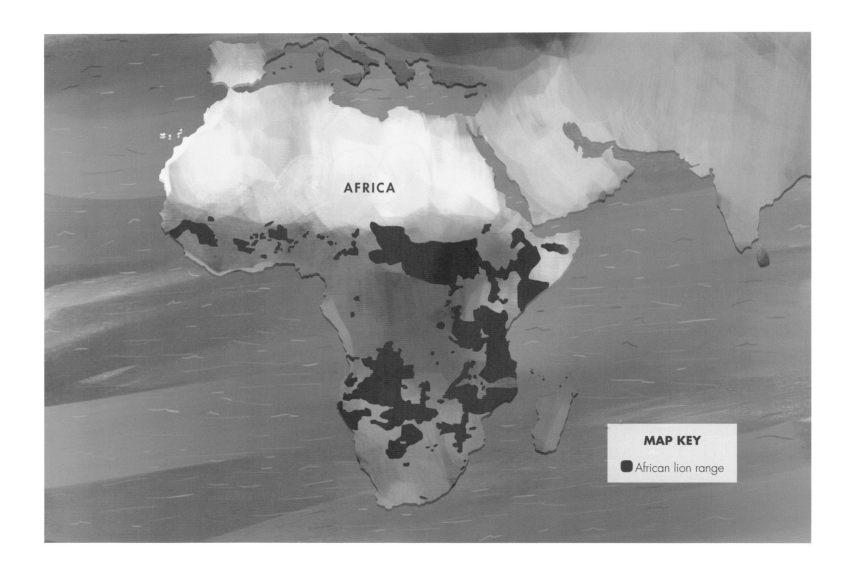

AFRICA

**MAP KEY**

● African lion range

# GLOSSARY

**Cape buffalo** A large, reddish-brown or black animal with curved horns that lives in Africa.

cub A young lion.

hyena A wild animal that looks somewhat like a dog and shrieks loudly.

**impala** A brown African antelope; the males have curved horns.

lioness A female lion.

night vision goggles Special glasses that allow you to see in the dark.

**pride** A group of lions that live and hunt together; one male and several females and cubs live in a pride.

safari An exploring vacation, often to look for animals. "Safari" means "long journey" in the African language Swahili.

## READ MORE

Blewett, Ashlee Brown. **Mission: Lion Rescue**. National Geographic Kids Mission. Washington, D.C.: National Geographic Children's Books, 2014.

Bodden, Valerie. Lions. Mankato, Minn.: Creative Education, 2010.

Ringstad, Arnold. Lions. Mankato, Minn.: Amicus, 2015.

Simpson, Phillip. **Lion Habitats Under Threat: A Cause and Effect Text**. Chicago: Heinemann Library, 2015.

Turnbull, Stephanie. Lions. Big Beasts. Mankato, Minn.: Smart Apple Media, 2015.

## WEBSITES

Lion | Arkive
*www.arkive.org/lion/panthera-leo/*
Watch videos of lions in the wild.

**Lion | The Atlanta Zoo**
*www.zooatlanta.org/home/animals/mammals/african_lion*
See photos and videos of lions at the Atlanta Zoo, and read some lion fun facts.

Lion Facts and Pictures: National Geographic Kids
*kids.nationalgeographic.com/animals/lion.html*
See photos of lions in the wild and compare their size to common objects.

Lion | San Diego Zoo Animals
*animals.sandiegozoo.org/animals/lion*
See photos of lions at the San Diego Zoo, and learn about lion behavior.

*Every effort has been made to ensure that these websites are appropriate for children. However, because of the nature of the Internet, it is impossible to guarantee that these sites will remain active indefinitely or that their contents will not be altered.*